The House of 12 Bunnies

Caroline Stills & Sarcia Stills-Blott

Illustrated by Judith Rossell

LITTLE HARE

www.littleharebooks.com

For David, forever ~ CS
For Gypsy, the chatterbox ~ SS-B
For Phoebe ~ JR

Little Hare Books, an imprint of Hardie Grant Egmont, 85 High Street Prahran, Victoria 3181, Australia www.littleharebooks.com

Text copyright © Caroline Stills 2011. Illustrations copyright © Judith Rossell 2011. First published 2011.

National Library of Australia Cataloguing-in-Publication entry

Stills, Caroline. The house of 12 bunnies / by Caroline Stills and Sarcia Stills-Blott; illustrated by Judith Rossell. 9781921714405 (hbk.) For pre-school age. Rabbits – Juvenile fiction. Lost and found possessions – Juvenile fiction. Stills-Blott, Sarcia. Rossell, Judith. A823.4

Designed by Vida and Luke Kelly Produced by Pica Digital, Singapore Printed through Phoenix Offset Printed in Shen Zhen, Guangdong Province, China, March 2011

5 4 3 2 1

In the house of 12 bunnies
it is nearly bedtime,

but Sophia has lost something.

In the kitchen
there are 5 cups, 4 plates, 2 bowls
and a mug without a handle.

Sophia hunts through the cupboards.

In the dining room
there are 3 highchairs, 6 wooden chairs, 2 wicker chairs
and a stool with a wobbly leg.

Sophia looks on top of the table.

In the living room
there are 4 trumpets, 1 piano, 2 drums, 4 violins
and a guitar without any strings.

Sophia explores
behind the piano.

In the playroom
there are 5 teddy bears, 3 dogs, 2 cats, 1 duck
and a giraffe with the stuffing coming out.

Sophia rummages
amongst the toys.

In the garden
there are 3 prams, 4 tricycles, 2 scooters,
2 pogo sticks and a bike with a flat tyre.

Sophia peers along the fence.

In the attic
there are 3 boxes, 3 suitcases, 2 trunks, 3 bags
and a chest with a rusty lock.

Sophia searches
between the boxes.

In the laundry
there are 7 buckets, 2 brooms, 2 mops
and a duster without any feathers.

Sophia delves into
the laundry basket.

In the bathroom
there are 4 spotty towels,
5 striped towels, 2 plain towels
and a towel with a big hole in it.

Sophia checks
around the bath.

In the bedroom
there are 4 single beds, 3 cots, 4 bunk beds
and a trundle bed without a mattress.

Sophia peeks
under her pillow.

In a warm, cosy
bed there are
12 snuggly
bunnies

and a
bedtime story.